THE NEXT DIMENSION

THE RIDDLE OF THE UNIVERSE

PRANAV SUNIL

DEDICATION

To my mother, Prathiba and father, Sunil. For raising me
to believe that everything is possible. You both are the
reason why I was inspired to write this book. Your
support of my writing means the world to me.

To all my teachers who have been my constant source of
encouragement to achieve new heights.

To my family and friends who have supported and
encouraged me to finish this book.

Contents

Also by Pranav Sunil

Thriller: Tales of Terror: Terror Redefined

Science Fiction: The Next Dimension- The Riddle of the Universe

Acknowledgements

First and foremost, I would like to thank my mom and dad for giving me this life filled with love and happiness. You guys have and will always be my pillars of strength. This book would not have come to its completion without them constantly pushing me and challenging me to give my best.

My grandparents, uncle, aunt, and my cousin sister who have been highly appreciative and enthusiastic to see my work completed.

Finally, to my best friends who have stood by me at all times and a big force behind me.

Above all, thank you God for all the wonderful and blessed moments of my life.

CHAPTER ONE

I rushed toward the end of the hall as I pushed out several students to move out of the way as I knew if I don't get to my biology lessons on time I would go to detention again. But the fact was I kind of preferred detention over my biology class as I hate biology class. I also hate the fact that my stepmother and my stepfather are going to give me the biggest lecture of all time. To give a background to my life my name was Kurg (I was adopted when I was a baby, and my stepparents apparently did not have any other better names for me) and I lived in 'The Normal Town' in a small state. Trust me the town was anything of normal. I hated biology and had an admiration for astronomy ever since I was a toddler. I remember when I was in 1st grade me and my peers went to a camp for 1 week in Canada. I remember waking up at night feeling disturbed and I wanted to get some fresh air. I still remember the smell of the Orchids and The Lilies blooming in the early summer. I stepped outside to breath the fresh air and as I looked up, I saw the most beautiful thing in my life. The spirals of the milky way and the stars and shooting stars. I stared at it until it faded into the light of the sun.

I ended up sleeping in the middle of eating my breakfast. I reached biology class in time and while I entered the door and was about to speak but Mr Alfredo cut me out and said, "You're in detention again Kurg. Go to the principal's office" I hate biology. I walked up to the door and knocked twice. "Enter", said a stern voice. I entered the room to see a young man, probably in his late forties with blue eyes and black hair looking down at me.

"What have you done today Jefferson."

"I was late to my biology class Mr. John."

"Again? Why were you late this time?"

"I was fixing the telescope in the science club during recess and before I knew I was half an hour late."

"Look. I appreciate your interest in astronomy, but you should also take interest in other subjects like biology. I know you are trying your best to be good but try harder. Your consequence will be either detention or a week's ban in touching the telescope."

"I'll take the detention please."

"Ok. You'll be in detention until 5:00."

"Ok Mr John."

"Off you go to your next class."

It was math, and it was another subject I really enjoyed. Before long it was time for detention, so I had to sit in a room and write a 5000-word text on biology. I sat there for 2 hours and got it done. I submitted it to Mrs. Kroger and went down the ground. The school was deserted with practically no one. The air was a little chilly and I hugged myself to keep me warm. As I reached the other side of school I saw a figure. It was a small girl with a ponytail and a pink barbie bag and a jacket on her. I walked forward and the figure seemed to be a little more familiar. I was right next to her when I realized that she was my stepsister

Kate and I had forgotten to pick her up from school as I promised. She stared at me while I was looking down at her.

"Are you gonna pick me or not."

"I'm sorry I was helping the teacher doing a project with the telescope."

"Your lying."

"No I am not."

"Who was the teacher you were helping?"

"Mr Robin."

"He quit last week."

"Mrs. Allison."

"I saw her leave an hour ago."

"Mr Brownie"

"He's our dog. Look do you want to tell me the truth or you want to keep on lying."

"Ok fine I was in detention for being late to biology class."

"Make sense. Anyways I'm going to snitch on you no matter what."

I groaned. I hate that evil creature so much. In a matter of seconds, we reached home. I unlocked the door and entered the house. I turned on the light all over the house and told Kate that I was going to freshen up. I climbed the stairs to the bathroom and took a relaxing hot water shower. I got dressed and completed all my homework. I made myself popcorn and sat down on the couch to watch some TV. After a few minutes the doorbell rang. I checked outside the peephole to see my stepparents waiting for me. I let them inside and my dad handed me a box of chocolate donuts. I grabbed it from him and started munching on it. Before I could even enjoy it, Kate grinned at me and said, "Mummy Kurg went to detention and forgot about me, and I had to sit there outside all alone, cold, waiting for him. I was so scared if somebody took me." She began fake crying.

My parents comforted her

"You shouldn't have left your sister alone Kurg."

"Why did you get into detention anyways?"

"I got late to biology class."

"Kurg your sister is right. What if someone took her."

"Not even 5 seconds later they'll return her."

"Kurg I am serious here go to your room."

"Ugh."

I ran up my room and sat there with my popcorn watching TV. My sister was very annoying, and I hated her. Then I got an idea. I climbed down the stairs and came up to my parents and said, "Kate has a secret stash of candy in her room, and I can prove it." I grabbed their arms and pulled it up to Kate's room and at the same time when I opened it Kate was eating a whole chocolate bar with a box of candy spilt out.

"Kate what is all of this?"

"Mom It's not what you think."

"Not a word you both are grounded. No going outside the house for a week."

"I smiled at her as I left, and she hissed at me. It was fun getting revenge. I came back to her room, grabbed a candy, smiled at her, and left. I played some video games for some time, and I heard the dinner bell. I ran down the flight of steps and came to the table. My mom set the table up and we began eating.

"I have something important to say."

"What is it dad."

"I got a new job in New York, and we'll be moving next week. I want us to appreciate this. I will be getting a higher salary. You'll both have huge rooms. We'll live in a three-story house and your own balcony."

"But dad I am just elected leader of the astronomy club for

a month.”

“Dad this is not fair I have so many friends. I don't care about Kurgs club, but friendship is very important.”

“The vans will be coming tomorrow and it's a nice place. You'll be in a wonderful school with good teachers, and you can focus on astronomy, and I am sure there will be new friends waiting. You can enjoy your lives better there. I just know it. Besides don't you love New York?”

“We do but our home is better.”

“We don't need to pay rent anymore we will have our own home.

We sat and ate in silence until my mom told something.

“We are moving into our old home. Where we brought Kurg into our family first. We decided to move to this town after that. You know what. Tomorrow, you say goodbye to your peers and come back and we'll all go to the mall here one last time to cheer you up.” The next day I packed up my bag and went to the Wilford school one last time. It was sad saying goodbye to all the teachers and students I knew because I was here practically my entire life, but the saddest part was saying goodbye to the telescope. It was a good one and I have seen many comets and stars with that. I gave my place to a child who really wanted to be the leader and said goodbye to my club. I attended all my classes in time, and I left. Then I waited with my sister until our parents came.

“Will you miss this school Kurg.”

“Of course I will. Why won't I?”

“How many memories do you have of being here?”

“Definitely more than how many braincells you have.”

She punched me in my shoulder and giggled.

“You know when you were born half of the doctors puked out seeing your face.”

"Hey that's enough ok. I know that I am very pretty."

"In your dreams."

"Look! Mom and dad came."

We entered our car and headed towards the mall. It was an hours' drive away. The ride was quiet until we reached there, and my sister was jumping up and down in the car seat. We went to the arcade and played a variety of games. We had too much fun there. I had some bonding time with my sister as we played a shooting game. We stopped the game after she got so mad that her face and a tomato had no difference. We watched a movie together and we had Pizza together at the food court. It was literally the best day of my life except the fact that I was leaving the town I lived more than half of my life and I was probably going to move into a place I absolutely loved. We weren't too rich but richest on the block and a three-story house sounds wonderful with the fact that I am going to have the best school in the world and live in the best state in America, according to my sister. I just knew that our lives were going to be perfect, and I guess I had to appreciate that. I only had vague memories of the place we lived but I knew it was a beautiful place with lots and lots of flowers and a amazing weather. There were palm trees that ran through the road, and we were facing the beach. I remembered my dad and I would run over the beach and watch the sunset together.

We drove back home, and we got packed. The next 2 days were packing and everything was being moved around. I knew that the next day I will be back in my hometown, the place that I was born and belonged to. I packed all the necessary items. I knew that this would be a new chapter for me and my family.

CHAPTER TWO

My alarm rang and I sprang out of my bed. We would be shifting from Texas to New York, and we had to go by road, so a long road trip awaited us. I checked the time, and it was 4:30. I freshened up and packed my final items. We bought another bed for all our rooms so this bed would be disposed. I got my sister to wake up and she climbed into the car in pyjamas, but no one cared. It was a long road trip to New York, and we stopped by many restaurants to get food. By then my sister vomited a million times because she had a ton of sickness and half of them were not to the open window right next to her but on me. What a brilliant choice. I changed three times because of Kate. Once I was sleeping and she woke me up and asked if I was sleeping.

"How is it going back there darlings?"

"Without Kate it would have been fine. Why did you take Kate along with us."

"Hey stop that Kurg"

"Stop fighting dears we'll be there soon so wait."

The wait ended soon, and we were out of the car in front of our new house. We could hear the roar of the beach not far behind. We stepped inside our villa, and it was luxurious. There was a huge TV and lots of plants. My bedroom had a separate TV 3 huge bookshelves and a huge bed. Almost all the bedrooms faced the beach, and it was beautiful. There was a fire lit and the barbeque was turned on and the waves were so elegant under the sunlight. The sound of it calmed my nerves. It was a beautiful house. There was a private library with so many books. There was a huge balcony in every bedroom and there were two treehouses built on two ends of the house for me and Kate and that was a huge surprise, and it was a huge tree house with a bedroom that was quite big for a tree house and a hall and a kitchen with working pipes and a balcony with a bean bag chair. I freshened up in a huge bathroom and got out of the house. I wanted to cycle around. I licked my lips and felt the sea spray on my face. I stumbled upon another boy around my age that is 13 fixing his geared cycle. I took a stick and came next to him and helped him fix it up.

"Thanks for helping me what's your name."

"Kurg, what's yours?"

"Mine's James. You gotta geared cycle too?"

"No I have an electric."

"An electric! There's only one person in my school who owns an electric cycle. He lives around here. He is very rich."

"You want to drive this cycle."

"Are you sure, because if I were you, I would let no one touch this cycle."

"Why is that?"

"This cycle is really precious."

"No worries. I have 3 more in the garage."

I saw him stare at me mouth open wide.

"Where do you live Kurg?"

"The house behind me?"

"How rich are you?"

"My dad owns half of the company that makes these big

houses for rich people?"

"How much is his salary?"

"I never thought of asking him that but I think its around 10 million."

"10 million! You're rich. Do you also live here?"

"No I just cycle around this community everyday to see this sunset."

"You cycle alone."

"Yup. All alone. There is barely any noise not many people live here."

"Can I cycle with you?"

"Sure."

We both cycled talking to each other about our lives. We had a lot in common at last I offered him a visit to our house for dinner. I smelt Barbeque from where I was. I let him inside the house and introduced him to my parents. By their reaction they were happy that I made a friend in 45 minutes which might have been a record for me because I don't make friends so fast. It usually takes 45 days to make one. The barbeque was delicious, and James really enjoyed it.

"Were do you go to school James?"

"I go to school at Henry Public Mr Jefferson."

"That happens to be Kurgs school maybe you could show him around the school."

"That would be a pleasure."

I took James to my room and he was astonished as it was quite big.

"Nice painting you have there Kurg."

"That the first ever picture taken of the Haley's comet that why it's small and on my desk. The one above is a portrait of Galileo using the first ever telescope.

"Wow."

"It's getting late my dad can drop you."

"That would be nice."

"Here take some leftovers for your mom and dad. I'll ask my dad."

My dad picked him up and dropped him at his home. The next day was a little bit of unpacking, and it was finally the school day. My dad dropped me at my school. People stared at me as I came in. I knew I was the new kid, but this was New York and there were kids everywhere. I saw Jason in the distance and waved at him. He saw me waved and came to me and grinned one of the biggest grins I've ever seen in my life.

"My mom was surprised seeing me come out in a Rolls Royce."

"Oh yea I forgot?"

"Do you want to see around the school. The observatory is just amazing."

He was right about practically everything. There was a huge chemistry lab and we happened to enter while a fire was starting to spread which was luckily controlled and there was a huge soccer, basketball and baseball stadium and a tennis field. There was a huge observatory, and the computer lab was just amazing.

"Look here Kurg that's Mrs. Parkinsons, our chemistry teacher and that is Mr. Julius, our arts teacher and look over there that Mrs. Opera, our music teacher and that is the principal Mr John standing there."

"Haha that is funny my old principal's name was Mr. John. He was a great man."

"This man is probably better."

"Anyways that Mrs. Freddie and Mr. Freddie both are the Maths and astronomy teachers respectively and look over there that baggie our biology teacher."

"Why do you call her Baggie."

"Keep it down she'll hear. Her real name is Mrs. Bag. Hence the nickname. Nobody is very fond of her, and I don't think she's even fond of herself. She's lonely."

"I feel bad for her."

"You shouldn't. She is very stern and if you are a minute late to biology class you are sent to 3 hours of detention."

"Oh that is harsh."

"Anyways you should probably collect your timetable and your locker information. You go to Mr. John he is right there and go now he is always busy."

I rushed to him immediately and stunned him. I introduced myself to him.

"You are Mr Jefferson's son right. Yes, I know him he and I studied together. Yes, here is your timetable and your keys to your locker. Its number is E10 right down the hallway and I suppose James has given you a school tour. He is a good guy. You should probably hang out with him. I am late I got to go. Anyways good luck for your school."

I rushed down the hallway to E10 and dumped my other stuff. I saw James waking towards me.

"You're E10 huh. I'm E9."

"What's your first subject."

"I have biology."

"Same. We better start walking there we need to be there early, remember?"

"Yup. Baggie does not like late children."

"You're right!"

"You know what makes me happy is that me and my sister don't need to go to the same school. She is in elementary thankfully. You know that your school is really crowded like my old school was almost always dead quiet."

"Not many people there huh."

"Not only that it was a very private school only some people got to go there."

"Sounds interesting."

"We are almost there just reminding you don't sleep in the class."

"Nice one I won't I promise."

"Luckily the biology room has proper coolers for the summers. Only some parts work now. There has been a slight problem of fungus growing on some parts of the ventilation. The spores got children sneezing a lot."

"Wow. How about these air conditioners."

"They are fixed. Anyways class is going to start in 15 minutes, and we have some time so take out the book which is green."

"That's funny I can't seem to find it."

"It's dark green and has an image of a plant in there."

"I can't find it!"

"You sure?"

"I am a hundred percent sure."

"Did you leave it in the locker?"

"I think I did."

"Go run and get to your locker, you can reach it in 5 minutes."

I ran really fast and got to my lockers and I couldn't find my keys and I was really panicking. I looked at it again and felt my pockets get heavy and felt my keys. I used them and got the books. I closed the locker and ran until I reached the room. I entered with the green book and some other random book which I took out just in case.

"Good thing you have reached."

"It could have been very scary if I was a minute late."

"I bet."

CHAPTER THREE

"Open your books, class, to page 72", said Mrs Bags. The sounds of rushed pages filled the classroom. Mrs Bags started to talk about connective tissue. As James said, the class was quite boring. The fact that we had already learnt this topic 2 years ago made it worse. Luckily the class ended quickly, and we could go to recess.

"Can I ask you something Kurg?"

"What is it, James?"

"Do you like to have some fun?"

"As in?"

"Like do something naughty."

"Like what?"

"You know what. Leave it. It is probably a bad idea"

"No let me. I like being naughty."

"Ok. Good to hear. The plan is to change the time of the clocks 12 minutes early."

"Why exactly 12 minutes?"

"You'll find out just remember to wait till 4th period recess. The teachers will all be out in a meeting."

"Oh that is why 4th period is free."

"Just remember to not be caught."

"The council roams the halls whilst the teachers are gone so we better be careful."

4th period rushed towards us. As the teacher started to wrap up, I felt my heart beating at 100 times a second. Don't worry I did not get a heart attack and my doctor says my heart is fine. Before I knew it the bell rang, and it was time for action. I looked at James and he looked back at me and smiled. I nodded. I did have second thoughts about the plan, but I wanted to have fun. I dispersed into the crowd, and I glanced at James one last time and we headed over to the staff room. There was no one there and we slowly started twisting the clock 12 minutes late. It was fun to do all this, and it really made me feel better after moving into a new house and adjusting with a new school. We silently made our way into the last cabin in the staff room. We twisted the minute hand of the clock and was finally preparing to leave. The doorknob twisted and the sound that we dread, the door slowly squeaking, and a boy few years older than us entered the room. He had brown eyes and brown hair and a stern face.

"What are you two doing here."

"Nothing."

"You do know that students are not allowed don't you."

"Yea. My name is James, and he is a new kid. He got lost and I found him in the staff room clueless where he was and just telling him the basics."

"Really. Then explain to me why the clocks are upside down?"

"We don't know."

"Tell me the truth or else you are suspended."

"Ok we did do it."

"Why did you. Are you here to make a bad impression?"

"We did it for fun."

"It is not fun anymore is it now. Why don't you go to the principal's office and hear what is needed to be heard."

"Ok."

"Do you not know how to apologize."

"We are sorry ok."

"Now go."

I really felt annoyed at myself. Why did I want to go do these unnecessary actions. Now I'll get in trouble on the first day. I felt so stupid. My sister was probably having the best day of her life."

"Don't be too hard on yourself Kurg."

"What's the point saying that now. We have reached the principal's office."

I brought my hand out and felt my sweat drip down my neck. The world around me seemed to go quiet and slowly I knocked on the door twice. They seemed to echo down the silent hallway. The noise seemed to grow and grow. The cold wind blew at my face. I thought if there was a chance I would reverse time and make things right. By now I would be in math class. My thoughts are interrupted by a stern voice.

"Come in."

James nodded, and we slowly entered the room.

"James and Kurg why are you here.?"

"We got into trouble."

"For what?"

"We changed the time of the clock in the staff room."

"Why did you do that."

"We changed it 12 minutes slower so that the teacher would be late and as per your rules a teacher is not allowed to teach his or her class if he is 12 or more minutes late."

"That is not right you know that."

"Yes we do. We just did it for fun."

"So don't do it again I will be calling your parents, and you might as well fix all the clocks."

"Sorry Mr. John, we will not do it again."

"You better not."

So we went down the hall toward the staff room and started fixing all the clocks. We both did our work in silence. The rest of the day passed on silently with nothing interesting except a growing headache. The day came to an end, and I saw my car waiting outside the gate for me. I slowly walked towards the car, opened the door, and sat down. I could see my dad staring at me through the rear-view mirror.

"How was your day Kurg."

"You probably know what happened dad."

"Yes, I heard. I know you might find it very difficult moving into a new house and probably starting a new chapter in your life but that should not get you in trouble or change your character."

"I know that dad I just thought you know..."

"Enough from you Kurg you only deserve a punishment. I know you are stressed so this time we are being a bit lenient with you, so we are lifting your punishment. We really want you to work hard in school."

I was really tired of the lectures my stepparents gave me all the time but this time I agreed with my dad. When we reached home, I rushed to my room and began writing my homework. I could hear my parents talking about me in the distance. Just as I completed my final bit of homework my dad entered my room.

"Kurg your friend James has come to apologize to you for dragging you into making trouble."

Slowly James entered the room. I told him to take a seat and I forgave him profusely stating it was also my fault. My mother entered my room and looked at me.

"Kurg could you go to the market and get a new clock for your bedroom. Your clock is not working."

"I don't know where the market is."

"I do. I can go with you Kurg."

"That would be nice."

"If you want to go you must go now boys."

"Hey can we go shopping at the antique store together Kurg?"

"That would be nice. Can we go there mom?"

"Ok. Don't spend too much money. Come home by 7, dinner will be ready by then. Why don't you have James over for dinner. I'll be making something nice."

"That will be nice Mrs. Jefferson."

I dragged him out of the house, and we hoped on our bike. I checked my clock, and we had a whole 3 hours of fun and 20 bucks in my pocket and James always had 5 bucks in his pocket. We reached central town and parked our bicycle outside the store and hopped inside. There were few people inside looking around. It was nice being in the store. The AC was turned on and the room cooled us off. The sun was showing its power although it was evening, like a candle that burns brightest before it burns out. I got myself a clock which was quite nice and told the shopkeeper I would pick it up after an hour and a half. He agreed and we hopped on our bicycles and cycled to the antique store. It was a pleasant store to be in. It had so many collectable items and James was a well-known customer. Half of the items were under 10 bucks and weren't that costly. We started to look around and I found a framed piece of old Victorian writing. I knew I had to buy it. We got what we wanted. James got a fishing hook. We decide to grab some snacks, so we got some fries and an ice cream with the rest of the money. I couldn't wait to put the frame on my study table. It was a writing about the Halley's comet, and I knew it was old and it might have been written by Edmond Halley himself. We picked up the clock and drove home. The sun was starting to set, and we had a lot of time free, so we came back home and climbed up the tree to the tree house and watched the sun slowly fade. We went inside for dinner. It was mashed potatoes, gravy, and chicken. After dinner me and James went to the tree house and spotted the constellations. It was very chilly, and frost began to form. Our house was on the far side of town, so stars were very clear. We saw Saturn through my mirror telescope that I won in a quiz. It was a good telescope.

"Hey stop poking me, James."

"I am not."

"Now you did it again

"I swear to god I am not touching you."

"Ok fine.

"Now why are you poking me Kurg?"

"Am not you were literally staring at me."

"Must be my imagination."

"Must be."

CHAPTER FOUR

It took 6 months after I moved into New York for everything to settled down. Me and James grew very close, and we became best friends. The last time I had a best friend was 7 years ago, but he left for Canada. I still remember how much I cried the day he left. My sister said I acted like a baby. The next week she and her best friends stopped their friendship and that led my sister to go to therapy for a month.

This week all I could think about was the alignment. All the planets of our solar system plus another 2 stars in a binary system would be perfectly aligned for 2 minutes making it one of the brightest alignments in the history of mankind. I knew I really needed to see this alignment not only how cool it will be but also the fact that I needed to write an essay about any topic and make a project on it. All I thought was this alignment. I knew that this alignment was only happening once every 22 billion years. The government would be shutting of all power in the city 1 hour before the alignment so everyone could see it clearly and it was luckily a bright and sunny day. The week passed by quite fast with not much happening. The last day of the week finally came and the next day would be the alignment. "Hey James are you excited for the alignment."

"Sure am."

"Like imagining being the lucky ones able to see the alignment after 22 billion years."

"Yup sure is exciting."

"You want to come to my house during the alignment."

"Yup."

"You know what. Let us have a sleep over."

"Sounds like a good idea."

"I know. You can bring the snacks."

"Yea keep the telescope ready."

"Yea and we can sleep in the tree house."

"Won't it be hot."

"It drops to like 15 degrees Celsius at night."

"Is that cold."

"It is very cold."

"Sounds awesome."

"And guess what. My dad got me a double lens so we both can see it at the same time"

"That's cool."

That day I came home excited and told my stepparents all about it. They were happy about it, and they said it was a good plan. We would be all alone in our house except with our sister because my parents would go to the public telescope as it was a huge one. The day flew by and the following day all I did was spend my time in the tree house setting up to the right altitude. I wanted it to be perfect. By then I decorated my tree house, and it was very pretty. I got everything set all over the house and my parents had asked to pick up James. I picked him up with my cycle and we cycled all the way back through the sunset.

" I am thrilled to see the alignment Kurg."

"Me too James."

"Don't you think it is a bad idea turning of all the power in the city."

"It is not all the power just a small amount in the lights. There will be lights in the hospitals and such important places but generally it is going to be pitch black except the moonlight."

"Sounds cool."

"It really is."

"I think we better go faster. An hour from now it is going to be lights out."

"Come on we are there."

We both parked our cycles and jumped out of them and ran towards the house and our parents were already out. I had to just take care of the house.

"Take your sister along Kurg."

"Mom she is going to ruin everything."

"You don't want to leave her alone in a dark house."

"She'll be fine."

"She'll be crying half the night. Please can you do this for me."

"But mom..."

"Kurg this is your last call take your sister or no sleep over."

"Fine."

"Good boy now have fun and we'll be back. Pizza will be here in an hour."

"Now we must take Kate along."

" I think we can handle her Kurg."

So we took Kate and headed toward the tree house and slowly the power went off. It was really pitch black.

"Has the alignment started Kurg."

"No it hasn't Kate. It will start in an hour."

"Then why did you bring me here so early."

"Do you want to be in a big dark house or with us."

"Ugh...fine with you."

"Then sit quietly."

"There is candy there and don't eat everything."

"Hey Kurg you locked everything right."

"I did Kate now keep quiet or we are going to put you down and pull the ladder up so you are stuck down and have nowhere to go."

"Ugh...I hate you."

I saw James smiling at me and I murmured to him about how my sister was like a steam engine train. Loud, noisy and something nobody uses or likes that much. Out of nowhere my head started throbbing like there were whispers in my head.

"Hey Kurg, I forgot to tell you, but I was just walking past your room when I noticed your new clock was acting weird."

"What do you mean."

"You know like your minute hand was kind of loose. Like it was wobbling between 8 o'clock and 4 o'clock and there was something off about the seconds hand, as in, like it moved slow, and it was moving fast again."

"That shopkeeper must have cheated me."

"That is the weird thing. That clock store is quite famous, and my mother adores its clocks. All our clocks are from there."

"Must be some mistake, nothing big."

"No that's the thing. I went into something called as the clock workshop when I was small and they showed this exact problem were either an invisible force trying to destroy you has possessed the clock or the gears are all messed up."

"I'll take the possibility that the gears are all messed up."

"Can you both stop talking about clocks and start like doing something related to the alignment."

"Talking of which I think it is almost time for the alignment. James you can look through here and Kate come over here and stand here. Can you reach there? Ok you can."

"I am supposing it is only a few minutes away."

"Yep."

I stared at it quite hard as I was adjusting the lenses.

"There you can see Mars Jupiter and Saturn and there's Neptune and Uranus."

"Yea I can see them they are getting aligned."

"3

2

1"

"Wow it is so pret..."

Just before I could even say anything, the ground started shaking heavily. My sister was screaming at the top of her lungs, and I was finding a way to keep myself stable. It was like catching someone on a moving bus.

"Grab on to me Kate."

"Kurg come on let's go down."

We rushed down the shaking tree and ran to the ground.

"I have never seen such a violent Earthquake."

"Let us stay here Kurg."

"It is to dangerous Kate. We don't know if the epicentre was in the ocean. If it was then we must leave now."

"Why is that?"

"We'll explain on the way."

"Take the bikes."

"Here James take an electric one."

"Isn't there any pink one Kurg."

"That is not what is important know Kate."

"I don't even know how we are going to ride when there is an Earthquake still going on."

"KURG, KATE I THINK I KNOW A SPOT OF SAFETY. SORRY I AM SCREEMING CANT HEAR YOU IN THE NOISE BUT FOLLOW ME."

"OK!"

We cycled at full speed and followed James.

"KURG AND JAMES CARE TO EXPLAIN WHY WE CAN'T BE NEAR THE OCEAN."

"KATE IT IS BECAUSE IF THE EARTHQUAKE IS ORIGINATED FROM THE OCEAN THAT MEANS THAT THERE IS GOING TO BE A TSUNAMI."

"KURG WE ARE ALMOST THERE COME ON. CYCLE FAST."

As we reached the shaking stopped and we reached a clearing.

"Hey Kurg just asking. I know this is dumb but is the earthquake because of you know..."

"It is not because of that. The gravitational force is too weak to cause a tide, but an earthquake is impossible. If there was one it could be detected."

"How isn't it impossible to detect."

"True but there is one way to detect an Earthquake before it strikes Kate."

James pointed toward a group of dogs in the distance howling.

"Dogs can detect the slightest shaking of an Earthquake but the dog next door a German Shephard didn't even budge."

"True Jason that means that means that the Earthquake happened so quick."

"Something that could literally only happen outside this world."

CHAPTER FIVE

Sirens roared across the city as people were under shock after the huge earthquake. Buildings were ripped apart and concrete was falling off. People were surrounded by the police and the paramedics. We climbed towards the town square. It was really a sight. Billboards were dangling off the building. The tall skyscrapers that took years to build were falling off as the police were still taking people away from the buildings, but more and more people were piling in. Out of nowhere the ground started to shake again and the people were screaming and suddenly from the centre of the city which was a clearing a fountain of hot water exploded from the ground shooting up several feet in the air. After people were seeing this more and more of the geysers started to form. The city was filling up with hot water when from a distance a man complained that his car was literally lifted up from the geyser.

"Look at how much pressure was there for the water to spring up the layers of concrete."

"Can we go home now Kurg."

"I think we should."

"Watch out James there."

Kate shouted at James as an emergency staircase collapsed on the ground. The top of the staircase was broken to form a hook that was tangled with a wire and when it fell down the wire broke and turns out the wire was connected to one of the main transformers and the transformers went out so all the power went off again and the city went black.

"I guess we should probably turn on our flashlight."

"We don't have one Kurg."

"No there is one on the cycle just click this button."

We cycled very carefully into our homes. I quickly checked the tree house which was surprisingly not that destroyed. I gave a quick fix to my telescope and rushed down the steps and to my house. I locked all the doors and all the windows, and I cleaned the house with the help of James and Kate. After we were done, I put Kate to bed and wished her a good night sleep. I was down the steps when I heard James talking to someone on the landline."

"Who is it?"

"My mom. She says she'll pick me up day after tomorrow. She is in my aunt's house in the other side of the state, and they can't come back till day after tomorrow."

"Why?"

"The city exit has been shut."

"Oh."

"Are you going to sleep Kurg?"

"No I will be waiting for my parents."

"Someone is calling hold on. It is your mom Kurg."

I went up to the landline and put the telephone up to my ear.

"Kurg are you all right."

"Yea we are fine."

"Listen we'll be back there by tomorrow morning. The police have shut the way back to our house."

"See you tomorrow then."

"Ok Bye."

I put the landline down and sat on the couch.

"You want to go to my room James."

"Yea."

"Come on."

"Hey Kurg, now that we are in your room can I check out your clock and try to fix it."

"Yea."

I took the clock out of the wall and gave it to James. He sat on my chair and laid the clock on my chair and took a pencil from my pencil stand and asked me for a screwdriver. He opened the battery frame and pull out the entire back of the clock revealing the working gears. He slowly started to dismantle the entire frame of the clock one gear at a time.

"You sure you know what you are doing James."

"I am."

He continued to remove the items and start to polish them with his handkerchief and put things back in place and looked at the front of the clock again and sighed.

"What happened James."

"The clock is perfectly fine."

"Then what is the problem."

"The clocks hands are still acting weird."

"What do you mean you just said everything was fine."

"The gears are perfectly fine and the mechanics are perfect and the batteries seem to be new and the hands are well connected to the gears."

He picked up the clock and handed it to me when all of a sudden the back frame of the clock fell of and left me holding the front face looking at the clocks handle.

"Sorry let me pick that up for you. I guess I forgot to screw it back on."

"James look at this."

"What."

"Look at the hands of the clock it's still working."

"That's right it is spinning but the batteries are not connected, and the gears have fallen off. Then how could it possibly be working?"

"Is the hands of the clock magnetic. Possibly there is a magnet."

"It is usually plastic or steel neither are magnetic."

We both sat in silence and looked at the clock. It was then I had a very bad headache. The sound of blood rushing in my ears was overwhelming and there were these strange whispers in my head that were so faint to hear separately but deafening together. It was out of these strange whispers that I had a vision of a crater and I felt like I needed something in that crater when a force started to pull me into the abys and I started falling an infinite hole. The vision changed to an old memory of me when I was five and my sister was a baby. I was reading this book about codes, and I started reading this highlighted line. *'Morse, binary or any other code can be seen in clocks ticking strangely, blinks of people when help is required or tapping of a table in strange patterns may suggest it be a code.'* I woke up from this vision to a strange feeling. James looked at me and frowned. I looked all around the room and was shocked to see my room was completely upside down. Books were scattered all over the room and items and decorations were down and chairs were flipped.

"What happened to my room?"

"I don't know. I went out to get a glass of water while you were meditating and came back to this."

"But I didn't even touch anything."

"Really."

"Yea. I was closing my eyes and were in deep thought."

I looked around the room and was surprised to find a

pattern.

"Look around James. There is something weird in this room."

"What do you mean."

"All the items in my room are scattered facing two things. The clock and the writing about the Halley's comet I bought from the antique store."

"You're right."

"I think I understood the clock problem."

"Good."

I looked at the weird clock one more time and I took out my computer and took out the morse translating app that I downloaded for no reason and I asked James to type out the symbols.

" -.-. .... . -.-. -.- .... - ....- .-.. .-.. . -.-- ... . -.-. --- -- . -.-.-.- "

"Ok it is saying check the Halley's comet."

"Why?"

"I don't know."

I picked up the old frame and looked closely at it. It had a small item that seemed to be protruding the writing. I carefully opened the frame to see that the paper was removed and revealed an old paper behind the sheet. I unwrapped the paper to reveal few coordinates

" 40°42'46"N 74°00'21"W"

"Let me just check that Kurg."

"Ok"

"Ok it is in New York and according to the google maps it is just a few blocks away do you want to check it out."

"Yes."

"Let me send the place to my phone." "Are we going there now? What about Kate? "She is a sound sleeper. We will leave locking the doors and come back quick."

We quickly went out of the house and down the road on our bikes. The air was fresh, but the buildings were still quite ruined. Luckily our house did not have much of a problem except a few broken vases and mirrors. We arrived at a clearing with few trees around us. A faint light was seen in the distance, and we followed it to an old tree. There was an old bulb hanging from it and it had lots of fireflies around it. With the help of the light, we were able to make a carving on the tree.

Alex Smith

123 Broadway

Apt. 45

47 W 13th Street

Unit 2A

Brigston

New York, NY 10011

"Well, we have an address."

"How are we going to get there James?"

"Why do we have to go there?"

"We have no other choice. There is something that is pulling us there and we need to go."

"How is that going to be Kurg."

"I have no idea.

CHAPTER SIX

"Why do you have to go there Kurg?"

"I have been getting these strange visions and I think it is pulling me towards something."

"As in what? Visions? "

"It is basically as if I was near a crater and I felt like I was finding something and I was being pulled towards a crater and I…"

"Fell off the crater to an infinite abys?"

"Yea how did you know?"

"Because I had that dream the day you arrived at New York."

"Look this is all exciting but I need to get there."

"That's the thing. Brigston is on the other side of town."

"We need to get there."

"Look we'll start tomorrow."

"Yea your right it is getting late."

"I am getting tired."

We cycled back home, and I let him sleep in the foldable bed. I got it set up for him and we slept peacefully.

The next day we had to make our plans. But it seemed impossible. We just had to wait. Jame's mother picked him up the next day and the day just went on normally. The next day was a working day, and we went to school. Every

Monday we had a homeroom session as we were technically part of a classroom. James was also in my homeroom so we could discuss about getting to Brigston. The talks slowly subsided as the teacher entered. It was Mrs. Ally and sheAlly, a very friendly teacher.

"Sit down class. Listen I've got some exciting new for y'all. Tomorrow we'll have a week's trip to the flower valley at Stonewood town near Brigston."

My immediate reaction was looking at James and he was looking at me. It would be a perfect plan to visit Brigston and visit the address.

"Class you only have half day today don't forget that. So, you'll be going home early today."

During recess and break me and James got to meet each other and decide on how to get to the address.

"See Kurg what if we get caught sneaking out of the rest of the gang. We will get into trouble like last time."

"We will do it at night that way no one will notice us."

"Good idea."

The day passed on like normal and my stepparents were happy about the fieldtrip and practically everyone was happy except my stepsister. All she did was complain about the fact that I was going, and she was not.

"Mummy how can Kurg go and not me."

"Kate, enough of this bad behaviour. One more word you are not going on your next field trip."

"But mummy look at Kurg. He is making a face at …"

"That is it you are not going on your next field trip."

Kate went off crying, and I was secretly very happy. That night I packed my backpacks with all my necessities. It was really going to be one exciting field trip and one stunning adventure. The next day I was up early and off to school. The early morning sun hit my face as the relaxing sound of the waves crashing onto the shore made me relax. I could taste the sediments of salt on my lip and soon I was in the city again. There were many parks all over the city and a cloud of smoke appeared onto my face as I breathed out. I reached the school and into my classroom. There were few students waiting there and finally James entered. He came up to me with a huge grin.

"Are you excited."

"Yup really excited."

Soon we were called onto the bus, and we were ready to go to Brigston. Soon we were riding on the bus and later I began to sleep during the trip. In the dream I was at a cabin in the woods with practically moss-covered trees all around. I had a lantern in my hand, and I opened the tall door to the cabin. I slowly entered the dark house to see it was just like a normal cabin but was on the verge of collapsing. Everything was rotting and the wooden floor felt damp. It was then the floor underneath me collapsed and I fell down the same hole into an abys. Light around me disappeared and the world above me was shrinking and shrinking. I felt like I was being consumed by a black hole until I felt the phenomenal pain in my head like an earthquake was ging on inside of it. The pain grew so hard that I woke up and startled James. I was in cold sweat.

"You all right Kurg?"

"Yea just a nightmare."

I decided to stay awake the rest of the trip looking down onto the barren land. Slowly the land started turning lush green with trees all around. The bus pulled over onto a small piece of land with a vast number of cottages stretching till the horizon. Right next to them was a series of strawberry plantation and the smell of strawberries filled the air. There was a distinct smell of mangoes as I slowly spotted few of the ripe ones on the trees. We made our way to the main hall. It was a very pretty resort. We were brought to our room i.e. one of the cottages and me and James would be staying together. We ate our lunch which was incredible with a variety of food. There were slices of pizzas, cubes of lasagne, mac n' cheese, spaghetti, turkey, mashed potatoes, cold chicken, gravy, cheese veggies and a lemonade. I had to try every one of the items. They were delicious. James made a sandwich out of everything and enjoyed his creation. I tried to do so and as I had my first bite one of the teachers gave me a side eye and as an excuse, I said I didn't like it even though I absolutely enjoyed it. We were stuffed after lunch and made our way to our rooms. James collapsed on his bed, and I sat on mine. I decide to go out for a walk to make me feel better. I went out to feel the fresh air. I took a strawberry and ate it. It was so good. I had one after another. I couldn't stop.

"Don't finish of the field."

"I looked behind to see a tall old man with a stick in his hand. His eyes were old and kind but shone with brilliance. His smile was wise, and his wrinkled face lit up. He had thin grey hairs that shone in the afternoon light."

"It's very good. How do you grow these."

"With love and dedication and of course water and sunlight."

I chuckled at his response.

"You know you remind me when I was younger. I used to love strawberries too and I went on a field trip just like yours and I ended up falling in love with farming and ended up growing around 30,000 strawberries every year."

"I guess they are a best seller."

His face was covered in a shadow."

"Unfortunately no. We can't sell it to the people outside

the town. My great grandparents owed the town millions of dollars and to owe them they gave these strawberries for free so that the town sells them to get money. The money was ours and we were supposed to have it but the frauds in our town thought different."

"Well why don't you go to court. You probably have your legal documents don't you."

"That's not how it was. They burnt our old house and everything in it but luckily the new mayor cared about us and promoted our business and he even reduced how much we owe them."

"Wow you have one good mayor."

"Haha he is really a jolly good mayor. I think you got to go kiddo. See you around."

"See you around Mr..."

"Mr. Elfwood."

"That is one nice name Mr. Elfwood."

He chuckled as he went. I went back to my room and shut the door. I turned around to see James' face.

"There is a small problem that has occurred."

"What happened?"

"If we need to leave, we need to leave now."

"What happened?"

He pointed toward the old and dark woods. There was aleave,erent vibe coming out of there. It was a place of mysteries. The old trees whispered under the canopy hiding away the sunlight. It was a place of gloom but also felt nostalgic. I felt as if there were creatures that led you towards happiness. The forest seemed...safe.

"The house is at the heart of the forest, and it will be too late if we don't reach there in time. We need to pack the all the items required ok."

"Have them packed here."

"This is probably where we find out what our whispers and dreams and strange happenings are from. We have finally reached the end."

"Let's go."

But James was wrong. This was not the end or anywhere near it. It was just the beginning. There was indeed a very stunning and enchanting adventure ahead of us. I knew that there is a surprise coming for us, one, you and I will be shocked to know.

CHAPTER SEVEN

We locked the door behind us and ran towards the strawberry field.

"Bend down James you're going to reveal us!"

"Ok. I am trying my best."

We slithered past the field as I plucked few strawberries on the way.

"Why do I feel that there are bugs all over me."

I shuddered at the thought of bugs crawling all over my body. We slowly made our way to the end of the field and down to the forest. The temperature dropped 20 degrees as we stepped inside the forest. The old oak trees hovered above us as we slowly entered the canopy. There were the sound of crickets chirping and an eagle soared above us.

"You know Kurg you really want to go to the address? I mean stranger danger."

"Didn't you tell me that once you followed a guy into a forest when you were 5 for like no reason."

"True but still."

"My gut tells me we have to leave."

"Well I don't trust your gut."

"Me too."

"Geez I really think these woods are haunted."

"Not going to lie but I think they are."

"That tree over there looks like its possessed."

"I know right."

"We have another half an hour of walking."

"I know right so keep walking."

"Ugh I for goodness sake if I am dying It is because of you."

"I didn't kill you."

"I think you will."

"Come on what can a forest do?"

Just as I said a boar came out of the trees and stared at us. Its face was fierce, and mouth was covered in drool.

"I think you said that too soon."

"I think I did."

"I think we should umm..."

"RUN."

We literally ran for our lives. We broke several branches, got our faces in several cobwebs, our clothes got stuck in protruding branches, we started to get more and more cuts and bruises and ran until there was no more paths and just a layer of trees blocking the way with thorns sticking out of them. I felt like the boars were going to attack us at any moment. Out of nowhere a powerful voice came out.

"Look here ugly face."

An old man came out of the woods with a red ball. The boar snarled at him and ran toward the red ball the old man gave a powerful throw to the ball and the boar went running after the flying ball.

"Now tell me what you both are doing here?"

"We were um l-lost."

"No you where not lost you came here for a reason."

"No we were lost."

"I know you Kurg and you are not supposed to be here and since you're here you have to come with me."

"How do you know my name."

"Come with me first."
"No first you tell me how you know my name then I'll come with you."
"Ok now stranger danger applies."
"Shut Up James."
"Ok I will promise that I'll tell you but first I need you to come with me."
I looked at James and he nodded his head and we slowly started to follow the old man into a house. I was stunned to see the house. I whispered to James.
"I saw this house in my dreams."
"Really!"
"Yup. It looked exactly like this."
He opened the door, and the old man nodded his head and told us to enter.
"Should we enter?"
"I don't know he did save us."
"Yea but still."
"Let's enter and see."
We entered after the old man and James pointed to a small placard on the house.
　　Alex Smith
Unit 2A
Brigston

We have indeed arrived at the destination. The furniture looked nothing like the dream. It was completely normal, and the floor wasn't feeling damp. The old man asked us to take a seat. Me and James sat close to the door, and I saw James putting his leg outside to make the door not shut.
"You can take your leg out I am not going to harm you and besides it is a manual lock."
James slowly took his leg out.

"Listen this may sound surprising to you, but I am your biological grandfather."

"WHAT!"

"No James I am not your biological grandfather I am Kurg's."

"How? I thought my parents died in an accident and my grandparents were dead."

"Well your parents are not dead, and your grandfather is right in front of your face."

"Where are my parents."

"They are probably in a black hole."

"WHAT!"

"How is that possible Kurg's Grandfather."

"You can call me Alex. Well to give a summary everything you know about the universe is probably wrong."

"I knew it."

"Well the fact that stars, planets and all the bodies and the stuff you see in telescopes are real the dimension of the universe is a lie. The 4 dimensions of the universe do exist but exist in different realms. It is said that all dimensions live differently and can't communicate but unfortunately that is a lie. We live with the 4th dimension."

"Wow."

"Not only that, travelling at 99.999% the speed of light is possible."

"So what are my parents doing in a black hole."

"When you were just a baby, in our lab we got a high amounts of radioactive plutonic substance as well as the fact that the universes momentum stopped thus causing high frequency wavelength to start shortening as the critical size of the universe started reducing drastically."

"English please."

"The universe is collapsing on itself", I had to pitch in cause

James was looking lost.

"There was one way to stop it temporarily and that was making the Neuon particle. To make that we require something called as the dimensional code or the quantum code. You can find that in the singularity of the black hole. Where the gravity is so concentrated that it has its own mass."

"But I thought gravity was a sort of energy and has no matter."

"You are partially right James but a newly found particle called the graviton can be formed in such cases. This is a rare type of particle that can travel through all the dimensions. But unfortunately, in black hole the singularity is practically invisible so we couldn't actually get it. All we are trying to do is to get your parents to safety. But there was one good thing. Your dad has found the solution to the problem. See we have found ways to communicate with the fourth dimension and study it. We used the fourth dimension to communicate with you because we needed you. Do you remember the clocks and the taps and the dreams. Those where signals transmitted on the level so low and high that can interfere with time itself and we used it for communicating through thoughts and feelings. But we realized that it was too dangerous. But it was already too late."

"But why me and how can we trust what you are saying,"

"I thought you would say that."

Alex brought us to one corner of the room and faced the wall.

"Eureka assemble."

After which an electronic voice sounded."

"Voice recognized. Eureka opening."

The wall opened revealing a long modern lab like lit passage with voices coming from the other side of the passage. We followed him down the passage.

"This is Eureka our lab where we our working hard on different universal projects."

We came into the end of the passage and a door opened and a huge lab was seen. It was like no other. There was a huge hole at the centre with people of different ages working on a huge circumferential machine around it.

"The reason we were worried about you was the fact that you would be going inside that machine."

"Why."

"Before in fact long ago when you were a baby in this very lab your father told the answer to the questions as to how we can take the dimensional code but after a huge explosion no one can remember it. Their brains were electrically stopped to see the memory but only one person was there to remember this and that is you."

"Why am I here then?"

"Because we think you can instigate the memory but first, we need to know if you are ready Kurg."

"I am."

CHAPTER EIGHT

"Are you sure that this works?"

"Trust us this is definitely goifirst, work."

"I hope so."

few of the scientist put a small capsule on my head and another on James'.

"Ok Kurg now I want you to relax and lay your head down on the bed."

"Can you tell me again why I am here again. I mean Kurg is here for a reason. Why can't you do it on him, why me?"

"Well you both have a synced brain which is quite rare. You were lucky to find Kurg. With the synced brains you can easily dig into his memories. His brain will be sending jolts to your brain to access the memories. But for that to happen Kurg must be asleep, and you must be awake."

The scientist slowly injected a liquid into my body.

"What is that."

"It's anaesthesia no I want you do is to count from 1 to..."

I was well asleep by then. I think the machine started to work as my head started spinning with old memories and visions and it was like my life was being re-winded. The more these memories came my head started spinning and my head started throbbing with pain. It was like a million needles were being stuck into my head and the more the time more the pain and I finally got my energy back and woke up. I got up and started gulping down air the same way what you do after coming out of a swimming pool. I was brought some water and I gulped it down.

"How long was that."

"Around 3 hours."

"Wow that felt like few seconds."

"Your unconscious state perceives time differently."

"That's why sleeping feels so short."

"True."

"Coming to the point. Did you get what you needed?"

"Listen kid. I'm sorry but we couldn't. We need you to activate it. James has looked at all the memories you remember. But to us, we feel it might not be possible. Scientifically it can take years of therapy to get around 5 seconds of a memory and only a quarter of the time people remember what happened."

"Oh."

"Don't worry there is still hope you can find that memory."

"Were is James?"

"He is sleeping. That really took a lot out of him."

"Ugh. I'm hungry is there anything to eat?"

"There is a cafeteria right around the corner to the left."

"You guys have an underground cafeteria too?"

"Yup."

"I'm sure there is rooms for each of you."

"Actually there are apartments not rooms. We even have a hospital and a daycare as well as a controlled greenhouse farm."

"I was joking. Are there extra rooms because I think we must stay here a bit longer."

"There is. One for you and one for your friend."

"Geez you guys have an underground city going on here."

"More or less."

"How did you make it?"

"It was an underground mine that was continuously bombed. We just renovated it."

"Wow is there gold all around here."

"It was a copper mine and this entire place is worth more than gold or diamonds."

"How could you afford all of this."

"Well we just sold all of the space debris that we collected with our harvester."

"How do you have an harvester."

"It isn't that complicated. We were able to send a machine with a huge net the size of the machine right there the big one and collect around 500 rocks."

"You mean that big hole machine."

"Yea the wormhole."

"What?"

Yea it is a wormhole simulator. They send light, charged particles to that hole which creates a huge magnetic field lining up with the black hole's and send a ray of gravitons to the black hole."

"What if the gravitons collapse?"

"They won't as we are creating a path through space time and not our 3d time."

"So they are stable enough."

"Yes. Are you sure you are ready to go?"

"To save the universe."

"Here is the thing you can't speak to your parents, however you can actually communicate with them."

"How is that possible?"

"To make your travel easier you are converted to a 4th dimensional being that way you can control your path. But you must use space time to communicate with your parents and the other member."

"One question how can their oxygen tanks be working?"

"Time has saved them. Time fluctuance. Your 14 years is their 1 and a half hours. Their tanks can last for a week."

"Well I must start searching my brains for that memory."

"Don't stress to much kiddo. You'll get there."

"Thanks for the support. I didn't catch your name."

"Annie Rodregus."

"Well Annie thanks for the support."

Annie smiled at me and left. My grandfather came up to me. "I know this is very hard for you with so much pressure. But this is for your parents."

"Yes Mr. Alex."

"Please don't call me Mr. Alex."

He nodded his head and walked away. After these two conversations with Annie and my biological grandfather I realized one thing. My grandfather didn't care about the universe. He cared about his family, but the scientists cared upon the universe. My family was worth the universe for me, but the universe was also as important. I couldn't believe that the billions of stars, planets, moons and even life depended on me. I thought if I ever got the code together my life would finally be at peace. James came up to me. I looked up at him and thought that even though it was just a few months since we met, we really had a good friendship."

"How is Mr. Universal doing."

"Not that great."

"Lot of pressure on Mr Universal huh. Its fine you'll get over it"

"Thanks for the support"

"By the way look at this. This glass box looks like nothing right but put your hands on the glass."

I did what he said. It was really hot and I couldn't even bare it for a second. It burned.

"Ow."

"I know right. This is Methanol fire. It is known as invisible fire. And look If I pour this saturated solution the fire is seen."

"That is cool."

"You seem like you are thinking something."

"Nothing."

I couldn't help about thinking about it. I knew something was pondering in my head. I took a sandwich from the cafeteria. I looked at my watch and nearly dropped my sandwich. It was already 12PM at night. I asked the keys to my room, and I just laid on my bed thinking. Until the thought came to my head again."

And look If I pour this saturated solution the fire is seen."
And look If I pour this saturated solution the fire is seen."
And look If I pour this saturated solution the fire is seen."
I got up my bed and screamed.

"I got it."

I ran to the lab with my discovery.

CHAPTER NINE

I ran down the hallway and came up to Annie.

"I remember now."

"What do you mean?"

"I got the memory of what dad said."

"What is it?"

"Something about a Protizon."

"Hold your horse did you say Protizon?"

"Yup."

"That name strikes me somewhere. But anyways good job we must tell the chiefs."

"Who are the chiefs?"

"Your Grandpa and Dr Albert."

"Like Albert Einstein?"

"Funny but no. He is Albert Cooper."

"Oh."

"Come on in right past here."

We entered a large room. It was filled with these strange items that looked like it belonged to a lab. There, my biological grandfather sat talking to another older man who looked few years younger to him. They looked towards me as we entered the room.

"He got it."

"He did?"

"I did."

"You did?"

"Yes. I remember now. Dad said that the only way to see the gravitational field or the gravitons was using something called as the Protizon."

My grandfather and the other man looked at each other."

"Should we tell him?", The other man said."

"We should tell him Albert."

"What happened?"

"Don't feel bad but it is practically impossible to get a Protizon. There is a one in a trillion chance that it is on Earth."

"But dad told it. It must have some meaning."

"It doesn't have any, now you can go back."

"I know it does."

"That's enough Kurg. Go to your room kiddo."

I couldn't believe that they didn't believe me. I just knew it was there. I know I needed to find it. I came back to my room and sat on my couch.

"What happened?"

"Ahh. WHAT ARE YOU DOING HERE."

"My room is being prepared. Till then I am bunking with you."

"Could have come with a notice."

"What happened. You seem dull."

"Well some people don't believe me."

"I do."

"Of course you do."

There was a knock on my door. I opened it and Annie was standing there.

"I believe you."

"What?"

"About the Protizon. I believe you."

"How do you? I am starting to not even believe myself."

"No look at this."

She entered the room and sat on my couch. She opened her laptop and started entering something on her keyboard. She turned the laptop and I read the headlines.

A strange crater found on the outskirts of Los Angeles. Surprisingly very radioactive.

"So, what's the big thing about this."

"There is only one substance that is radioactive."

"Protizon!"

"Yea!"

"Are you sure."

"I did more research. It is transmitting strange light from it, representing, guess what. The Earth's magnetic field on that area."

"No way so it might be true."

"It is. I just know it."

"Tell the others we should leave immediately."

"There is a problem."

"Oh come on!"

"We can't tell Albert."

"Why is that."

"Nobody really trusts him. He left long ago in fact he was fired but he suddenly decided to come back a day after the crater was found."

"When was the crater found?"

"Last week. February 21, I think."

"Hey Kurg I recognize that day. The alignment, remember?"

"And the strange Earthquake."

"The Earthquake was actually caused because of this crater. The strange part is that we didn't find what hit the ground. We only found the crater."

Probably it dispersed all over the ground."

"That is a possibility. But first we need to figure out how to leave."

"Just sneak out. That's not a big deal the big deal is getting to Los Angeles."

"I already have your tickets ready, but the thing is that you should not be detected by the security breach. Your grandpa doesn't want you to leave."

"Then how do you get out."

Annie pointed towards the vents.

"Are you sure."

"You can do this. I'll send you all the details after I drop you at the airport. You go through the vents, and I'll go outside through the passage. You come out to the clearing."

"Ok."

"Good luck."

"Come on James lets go."

We climbed up the vents. I couldn't help thinking that from a small clock issue we reached the state of saving the universe.

"Are you excited?"

"Very much."

"But I still don't get why my grandfather won't let me leave."

"Maybe he is worried if you'll get in danger."

"What danger? The universe is ending what else should we do. We all would be in danger."

"Maybe he is just looking out for you."

"I don't know. Anyways I think we reached."

"Ouch you're stepping on my toe."

"Sorry."

"Here I'll pull you up."

"I can climb up."

"Are you sure."

"Yup."

"Ok. Annie's car is there let's go."

"I can't believe we are going to finally get what we need."

"You know the teachers are probably wondering where we went."

"I didn't think of that but who cares."

We got inside the car.

"You know you both should probably get some sleep. You haven't slept in a long time and the airport is quite far away so get some z's."

"We'll try."

There was too much adrenaline in my body, and I honestly didn't feel like sleeping until the ride picked up speed and a wave of tiredness hit me, and my eyelids started to get heavy. I was looking at the beautiful countryside. My eyelids slowly started shutting and before I knew it, I was well asleep. I had the same crater dream and this time the crater wasn't an abys but was normal and filled with Earth. There was a strong sulfuric smell and smoke erupting from it. There was a ball of rock that was glowing ice blue. It was chipping off and it slowly started to disintegrate. The light started to shine very brightly and began filling my entire view and I felt a tap on my shoulder, and I woke up to James tapping my shoulder. I got up drowsily and stepped out of the car and stretched. Before me was a huge lit up airport with noise all over from inside.

"Here, I have sent all the details to your mobile phone and here is a credit card. In case it runs out call me and your plane departs at 6 AM and your plane will depart at Gate 6. Good luck. The check in will be easy. You have flown before, right?"

"Yup."

"Good luck don't miss your flight."

"Thanks Annie."

"Now go."

We rushed to our terminal and entered the bustling airport.

CHAPTER TEN

There was a huge vibration. The engines roared its greatest. The airplane started speeding and the G force started increasing, as the speed started increasing and increasing. My adrenaline levels were high, and I couldn't even hold my excitement back. The plane started increasing speed until the runway started speeding away beneath us and before I knew it the nose of the airplane lifted, and we were airborne. The city started shrinking. Until it was finally a small dot. I really couldn't believe it. It was one of the most exciting things in my life. Until the plane started turning and my stomach fell like it came up to my throat.

"What will you like to order?"

"Umm I'll get the chicken sandwich, a hot dog, instant ramen and a chocolate milkshake."

"Ok that will be 28 dollars, and for you."

"I'll just have a chicken sandwich."

"That will be 7 bucks."

"Here's our card."

"Ok and, here you go."

"Thank you."

"James are you trying to order one of everything."

"Sort of. I'm hungry ok."

"You'll be too full later on."

"Who cares?"

"James it's a 5-hour flight."

"Make the best of what you have."

" Now I'm concerned if you'll finish the entire card."

"So? Annie said she'll refill the card."

"Imagine you in Annie's place."

"I'll happily give all the money."

"No you won't. From now on you'll eat whatever I order."

"No you can't control me."

"But I can take this from you."

I snatched the credit card from his hand."

"Hey!"

We had our food in silence as we heard the engines roar outside. I couldn't help but look at the clouds outside the window. It was like islands in the sky with the surrounding being an ocean of emptiness. The sky was still waking up from its slumber as the orange started to slowly fade into the blueness. The ball of fire stood proud above all, shining at its greatness. The hours passed slowly and the plane at last started to descend. The booming city of Los Angeles was visible but still the cars and the highway looked like toys from the airplane's view but certainly very eye catching. The plane made its way to the runway and landed with a violent shock. The vibrations were tremendous, and the airport slowly came into view.

"Finally we reached. I thought I'd die of boredom."

"Come on."

"Its actually quite hot here isn't it."

"It is surprisingly."

"Annie told that her friend would pick us up."

"Let's first try to navigate through this airport."

"I think the exit is there."

"Oh yea."

We made our way outside into the beating sun. People were holding posters all over the place and we navigated our way to the end of the line to see a board.

James and Kurg

"I think we found our guy."
"Yes we did."
Behind the poster was a woman who was probably in her late 40s and crazy blond hair. She had a mandala costume on and looked like a fortune teller. Her neck was adorned which beads of different stone one with a lapis lazuli, another with amethyst, and another with rose quartz and one with jades. Her earrings were big and bright and her face was lit up with joy and her blue eyes sparkled.
"Are you Ceser."
"Yup I am Ceser and you both must be James and Kurg."
"Yes."
"What interesting names."
I knew that phrase was directed at me and I just bit my lips and looked away.
"My cars over there now rush along otherwise I have to pay an extra 10 dollars for the parking time."
We rushed towards the end of the parking space where her brightly decorated pink van stood with these crazy tribal decorations all over the face of it.
"You can take shotguns."
I climbed into the front of the truck which seemed pretty normal except the fact that there were a million wobble head on the front of the car. I thought the back would be better but when I looked I almost fainted. There were pink LED's all over and the cushions were pink too. The place was covered in stickers and painted with hot pink. There

were pink freezers, pink blankets and a one of the hugest and pinkest teddy bears in the world. The windows were even stained pink and a bright colour of a mandala. I was shocked to see a Maltese dog which had its end of its fur dyed with ice pink. I looked towards James, and he winced at me.

"Hey can you do me a favour and give Doodle Doo his biscuits. It's right over there in the corner. 5 will do."

"You named your dog Doodle Doo?"

"Yes I did and I love her."

"She is very cute."

"You boys hungry."

"Surprisingly yes."

"I know a good restaurant here in the city you'll love it."

"So Mrs. Ceser."

"Oh just called me Ceser."

"So Ceser where do you work."

"I work at the Eureka Lab."

"I thought that was in New York."

"No kiddo its all over the country and all over the world at least most of the world around 95% and the rest are just research sights."

"Hey Ceser its me James from the back. This dog is looking very suspiciously at me, what should I do?"

"You should lay it on your lap and feed it by hand."

"What if she bites me."

"She usually doesn't do that to me, but I guess its pure luck."

"Hey Kurg. Next time I'm taking the front seat and Ceser do you mind noticing that you're driving a hundred miles per hour on a road with potential traffic."

"Listen kid I have 45 years of experience driving."

"How old are you?"

"46."

"Now my chance of living dropped like... a hundred percent."

"Don't worry I think I know how to drive."

"OH MY GOD THAT CAR WAS A CENTIMETRE AWAY FROM US!"

"So?"

"We could've died."

"I think the airbag still works."

"Have you used it."

"Of course I do. Twice a day."

"What!"

"Just kidding. Relax I'm good at driving."

"Why is this dog licking me?"

"We'll either it likes you or it's just thinking that it can soften and tenderise you so it can chew on you easily."

"Is there a cage for it somewhere?"

"The truck is its cage. If you want, you just turn it upside down and put it on the ground. It forgets how to get up sometime."

"Ok. I guess that works out."

"And don't tap its nose it remembers how to get up after that."

"Ok?"

"We reached now."

We reached an old restaurant with a 1950's style. We got in and I was immediately hit with the smell of old damp wood. We got our seats and ate our food and left surprisingly fast. It wasn't that the food was bad but the fact that it gave bad vibes.

"Y'all enjoyed the food."

"Yup."

"My favourite place I go here every week. So do you want to go to the crater or my house to freshen up?"

"Well we will be here only for 12 hours, and we have to go today but I guess we could have a nice shower."

"Good its right this way."

We rode around 10 miles and reached an old house. I was honestly surprised it looked ordinary and surprisingly quite nice. It wasn't even pink. We entered the house, and it was giving a sort of hibbie jibbie vibe but we managed to freshen up.

"Are you ready to go to Eureka?"

"I though we were going to the crater."

"Outside vehicles are not allowed only Eureka busses."

We drove an hour to Eureka which was surprisingly very much open compared to New York's. We came up to another employee.

"They've come here from Eureka in New York. For the crater."

He looked at us and looked at Cecer.

"Id?"

"Here."

"How about them?"

"They are from Eureka New York. He is the grandson of THE Alex Smith."

"How about him."

"He's accomplice."

"I don't trust you. I need Id."

"I told you."

"Sorry I can't allow you both."

"Ugh. Come on Jared trust me."

"Sorry no."

I was thoroughly annoyed.

"That's it. I know about the black hole, 4d attachment, the wormhole, the black hole, the Quantum code and the last piece to our puzzle is right there in the crater and we need to go."

"And besides we can fire you."

"Ok fine."

"That's what I thought. Good job boys."

"Sorry but you both have been manually denied from entry."

"What do you mean?"

"A member has raised suspicion against you so we can't let you both enter. You really need to leave."

CHAPTER ELEVEN

We backed off and we had a group discussion.

"Who could've done that."

"I think it was Albert. Annie did say he was suspicious."

"You're right James, I think its him."

"Why does Albert want to close it off so badly."

"Listen kids ,what you want, the Protizon is the most expensive item in the world and if you sell it you'll practically have all the money in the world."

"So thirst for money is the reason."

"We need to stop him."

"Most importantly get the Protizon. You have everything ready, and all the materials needed to collect it."

"Yes."

"Listen to me very carefully the Protizon is not where you think it is."

"Where is it?"

"Come here."

She whispered practically the most important part of the entire mission. It was surprising for both of us.

"You need to get there somehow."

"Before that does Albert know about this?"

"Probably not. Only few know about this that is me and 4 other dogs."

"How do you know this."

"Because I got to know this by a late scientist, and I still have the report. Nobody else knows about this report, him or what I told you."

"We really need to get there before him."

"You really do."

"But how?"

"Do you know how to fly a C16."

"I do. I went to aerodynamics club and practiced it a million types."

"You went to an aerodynamics club James?"

"You need to go right now."

"Where?"

"A C16 is right there."

"What!"

"Go. I'll distract them."

She took a huge stick and hit a button which supposedly started an alarm. The person named Jared who we were talking to earlier started screaming."

"Hey get off there."

"No I won't."

"Command infiltration."

Lots of security started coming and started holding her.

"Doodle doo come help me."

Doodle Doo jumped out of the van and started biting the soldier and Ceser started pointing at the C16.

"Come on Kurg we have no time"

We hopped on the flight. James started to pluck few switches and the engines started to roar. The plane started to jerk forward. The speed started to be increasing. The air roared in my ear.

"V1"

James shouted as the nose of the plane started lifting

forward.

"Airborne we are!"

"Woah this is cool."

"Shut the door oxygen is escaping!"

I closed the door and we flew high in the air up the layer of thin cloud.

"Keep it low James."

"I am trying the flaps are jammed it's only going up and down."

"What should we do?"

"I don't know. I can see the crater from here"

I noticed something from the corner of my eye. It was black in colour and there were 3 of them.

"Those are parachutes Kurg we can get off using them"

"Let me check the manual it says to sky dive and then pull on the left rope."

"Let's go we have exactly 30 seconds before we reach the ground."

We quickly put on the parachutes and opened the door looked at each other."

"Ready?"

"Ready!"

"Go!"

We jumped of the plane and started flying down.

"Pull on the left rope"

In a matter of seconds two huge blankets covered the sky. The descent was slow and the pressure on my back was increasing drastically. I looked down and saw the huge crater becoming larger and larger and we slowly landed on the ground the parachutes falling over us."

We released our extremely heavy suits and climbed out of the parachutes. There was a distant explosion in the distance.

"Well there goes the airplane. I didn't know how to land."

"What if the flaps were perfectly fine."

"Probably end up like that only."

"You know I really don't like your honesty."

"Not my problem."

"We need to get to the Protizon."

"Not so fast."

We turned around to see Albert Cooper smiling

"Why are you her Albert?"

"You know why I am here."

"What do you want?"

"The Protizon. I'm here to have it."

"You can't take it."

"I'm afraid I can and I have to ask you to leave."

"We won't."

"Security."

"Nothing can stop us."

"But I can."

A couple of men started coming towards and hauled us away.

I whispered to James.

"Start collecting the leaves"

"Distract them Kurg."

I ran into the crater and James tossed me a dust bomb and I threw it at the ground. Smoke erupted from the ground and spread miles above the air and into the forest.

Probably if seen from an aeroplane it would look like a volcano erupted emitting blue clouds everywhere. I broke into a heavy cough and so did everyone. I felt a hand grab me.

"James? It that you"

"Yes. Come on Kurg."

He dragged me to an open area, and I could see a

silhouette of a car. We got inside and it was already layered with blue dust. We shoved it of the seat.

"Where is the wheel."

"I don't know."

"Voice recognized Eureka activating. Base camp search. Trail found."

"Oh that's how it works."

"Eureka suggests putting on the seatbelt."

We strapped ourselves and the car lunged forward pushing us back. It was moving at such a great speed. I managed to look out of the window, and I saw that the car was speeding up but the smoke was chasing behind. It was speeding up drastically. We reached in a few seconds. We got off and ran towards Ceser. She saw us and ran towards us and asked us to follow. James jumped into the back seat and the dog jumped. James closed the door and I followed into the front seat.

"Which bomb did you use?"

"The big bulky one."

"THE BIG ONE? That expands a 10 miles radius. We need to ride fast!"

"Uh guys I can see it come towards us it's like 50 meters away."

Ceser pressed on the gas and the car sped away. The smoke was running a race with us now and currently we were in 1st place. The amount of smoke was huge for such a giant ball.

"You have the leaves don't you James."

"Safe and sound."

The reason why we took the leaves and what Ceser whispered to us is the fact that when Protizon comes in contact with the ground it heats up to form the waves but later it heats up so much that it becomes gas and since that morning was cold the Protizon condensed and the sediments were on the leaves. There would be just remains of the body that hit the ground, but the Protizon were on the leaves.

"The smoke is far behind now."

James took out one of the leaves and I saw a blue spark it was glowing, and the leaf turned blue.

"The heat from your hand is causing the reaction. I think we need it to be cold."

"Put it in the freezer."

James opened the mini fridge and put it inside.

"To the airport right."

"You guys hungry after the adventure."

"Yup!"

"Theres's food in the back."

James handed me a chips packet and a salami sandwich, and we devoured it. Slowly the airport came into view."

CHAPTER TWELVE

The plane slowly descended, and we were back in New York. It was good to feel the slightly cooler air. We met Annie at the Arrival area."

"You got the Protizon."

"Yes we did."

"Good because While you were inside the airport I saw Albert enter."

"Turns out he was really trying to get to the Protizon to sell it."

"For money I suppose."

"Everything was about money."

"I guess now we should fire him."

"I think we should suspend the entire Los Angeles Eureka."

"That's enough of enemies you've made for one day."

"But still they were very rude to us. The did not even allow us to enter. We ended up having to fly a plane. Go skydiving. Even throw the largest smoke bomb on the planet Earth."

"Wait what."

"Yea you gave us 3 bombs."

"Oh god I gave the wrong smoke bomb."

"What did you give."

"The last smoke bomb in the world. It takes around 5 hours

to settle down."

"It probably did by now."

"Was it cool to see the smoke come erupting."

"Was it dangerous?"

"No it is completely safe and ecofriendly."

"Good I thought it was a bad idea to use it for a second."

"It helped right."

"It helped a lot. How long does it take to make one again."

"Around 3 years."

"Oh no we are so sorry. We should have used a small bomb. We really are."

"Its fine. It helped right."

"It did."

We rode in silences back to Eureka. We entered the Lab again. It felt good to be there again. I could finally solve this mission.

Where have you been Kurg. I was so worried about you."

"Don't worry grandpa the Protizon is right here."

I took out the leaf.

"Where? In the leaf ?"

Slowly the leaf started to glow a beautiful combination of dark blue, baby blue and ice blue. The Gravitational waves started glowing. It was an aurora borealis in my hand. Everybody in the lab stared at us.

"You actually have the Protizon."

"Yes. Now we can finally save the universe."

"Now everybody work hard we need to finish the hole by tomorrow. Everybody works faster. FASTER. Jason take this to the lab and make it a little more stable. We can finally go to the black hole."

There was excitement everywhere. I explained the entire adventure to him. He was clearly disappointed with the fact that the person he trusted was against him.

"Do you think he'll come back."

"Probably not."

"Don't be sad. He was always bad."

"I'm not sad just that he has accomplices."

"They're probably there still digging."

"Not there, he has friends around here."

I stood still in shock. We weren't done with. I was completely shocked wondering what was going to happen. It was then an alarm sounded.

"An intruder has entered the breach chief."

A voice sounded.

"Eureka initiating self-lockdown. Preparing evacuation systems. Doors closing initiated self-powers system at enemy. Entering locks and shielding acti..."

The power went, and the lights went off. The emergency exit's light was turned off too.

"Come everyone this way."

A man shouted pointing his flashlight. Everyone rushed towards the exit.

"Come on Kurg let's go."

A wave of anger hit me.

"I'm not going. I must protect the Protizon and the machine. I need to protect Eureka. I am not abandoning the mission so fast."

"If he's not going, I am not", James shouted.

"I am staying", Annie shouted.

"If they want to protect Eureka they can but we are going", said some voice

"No if my grandson will do this for my family I will also stay."

My Grandad looked at me.

"You know what I'll stay."

"Me too."

"FOR EUREKA!"

People came back and started taking back up taser gun and put it up in all directions with me and the Protizon in the centre. An alarm sounded again, and the doors broke loose, and people came in and they had their own tasers.

"Don't make me do this Albert."

"I won't"

I looked at everyone, person by person. I felt weak and tired and stepped back and sat down and I had another vision. It was my dad talking to my grandfather.

"So it is the Protizon is it?"

"It is but there is a problem if the Protizon is accelerated in can cause a huge fire."

"Lets put it in a good container then."

"Good Idea."

I woke up and the sound of breathing was only heard and the tension in the room grew and slowly I realized a shot had been fired and people started shooting and people fell from both sides and I looked at the 100 bottles of extracted Protizon. I threw some in the air. They started to accelerate tremendously fast. The moment they hit the ground, the ground was on blue fire. I never loved fire this much. I saw the people from the other side started falling. I threw more and more until the room was almost engulfed in blue fire. Slowly the shooting started dying down and the room was only filled with people coughing. People were on the ground and the medics and military entered. I felt so tired and exhausted, and I slowly felt so weak and fell to the ground. I woke up in a hospital. A nurse was treating my burn wounds and James was next to me. He was having a nurse banding his ankle. He looked at me and smiled."

"Hit 15 people and got a taser in my ankle by Albert himself."

"Oh god, are you all right?"

"What do you think. It was a good idea causing a fire. How did you know about it?"

"A vision."

"Strange."

"Why?"

"They said that the visions were being controlled by Eureka. Then who did it this time?"

"Well that's another mystery to be solved."

My grandfather came to me. He had a covered wound on his right hand.

"Well good job kids. The fire was amazing, and your shooting was good James. I could only shoot 2."

"Maybe you can take classes from him."

"Ver funny. Hey here's the thing. The wormhole machine is ready and tomorrow you can go. Are you ready for it?"

"Probably not. A week at max the wounds need to heal."

"What was I thinking you're right. Take the time you need."

The week flew, and I was very much healed and before I knew it the day had arrived. I had a talk with Annie that day.

"You're stressing out too much. You must relax and remember you have already made it so far. It's just a step away to seeing your real parents and getting to save the universe."

"You do realize that you're making me more scared."

"Sorry about that. But you still must end up doing these things right."

"Of course I know. But what if I mess up."

"You can't mess up. You won't be able to. Remember you are traveling through in 4th dimension, and you are part of it."

"True."

"Don't worry. You can do this."

"Thanks for the support."

"No problem."

"How is your arm anyway."

"Getting better."

I put on my helmet and entered the lab. The rest of the people were on the other side of the lab. Every single person in the lab was looking at me. A voice came in my helmet speaker."

"Are you ready Kurg, this is me James."

"Initializing Magnetism."

The wormhole machine started pointing rays of energy right at the centre and the light grew"

"There was wind shaking everything. It was really like I was in a tornado. I took a deep breath and entered the light, and I was slowly engulfed by it.

CHAPTER THIRTEEN

Being in a wormhole isn't what you think it is like. But it is also very imaginable. It's basically light first and the more you progress the universe is seen but very twisted. It's like a fabric covering all around that is made up of Galaxies. The more you progress you start to speed up. I felt the fabric and it felt like nothing and everything. Strangely I could see the turns of the fabric itself. The fabric felt like liquid. It was literally like when you put your hand into a moving river. I put my hand outside, and it felt like nothing at all. My hand felt like air. In a distance I could see a small dot. An extremely small dot. It was completely black. Like the blackest black I have ever seen. The dot started growing bigger and bigger. I soon realized that that would be my destination. The dot started growing bigger and bigger until my eyes could detect its disk around it. I felt the fabric bend significantly around it. I just thought if I could just move the fabric I could bend some space. I felt like while thinking that I had to put some effort and when I looked at the fabric it was wider. I realized I was in the 4D world in a 3D body. I realized I could control the 4D world with my mind not my body. As I realized this the dot grew huge and my speed started increasing. I felt like I was traveling at the speed of light which would be physically impossible, but I entered the dot, and it was an abys. A black hole. The universe above me started growing small just like my dream. It felt like I was free but trapped. I knew that this was the place where the Gravity bends the fabric, where practically you had a hard time escaping. I knew now I wasn't in the black hole I had become a part of it. I looked up and saw the universe had become a small dot. It was shrinking above me. I felt relaxed. The most relaxed I had been in years. I felt myself slow down. I saw a group of humanoid figures. I walked on the fabric towards them. They seemed like humans. Now I could see them as I came towards them. I knew they couldn't see but I still tried. There was a man with brown hair and brown eyes and decently tall and other woman with green eyes and blonde hair. There was another man with black hair and black eyes and was very tall and another woman with white hair and black eyes and looked unique. I saw that their mouths were opening and closing, and I knew that they were speaking and tried to speak to them, but I forgot I was still in the 4th dimension. I used my mind to project a thought.

"Eureka has come to you, and we have what you need. Trust us."

They all looked confused and surprised. I knew what had to be done next. I got to see the singularity. I could feel it. I just new it was there. I slowly felt the Protizon in my bag getting heavy. I got it out. The Protizon was still very much in the 3D world. I took it out and it floated towards the singularity. The humans started looking at the Protizon that was lit up (I don't know why I call them Humans, but I was getting 4D vibes from the place, so I felt like an alien to the 3D world.). The Protizon started making its way to the singularity. It started wrapping itself around a huge singularity. I added all the rest of it and the entire sphere glowed and out of nowhere a ray of light shot up and came back down. It was crazy to see this happen. Their faces lit up as they saw this. Another loop of light appeared, and the whole black hole lit up as I saw it. They made their way to the singularity. One of the ladies took out a sphere and pointed it to the lit of sphere. There was a laser like light from the singularity to the sphere. Slowly the Sphere started shrinking and it slowly became nothing. I felt a shake in space time, and it was collapsing and moving upwards. I realized how important this was. The black hole was decaying extremely fast. I knew I had to get them out of there as soon as possible. I tried my best to ask them to move. I finally projected a light into their vision and tricked their brains into following it. The followed me through the other end of the black hole and back towards reality. Back towards home. They started following me back through the wormhole. I forced the block in my head to move and we were sped up the other direction, back home. The light I saw started growing bigger and bigger and we were finally in the light. I felt myself again. The no gravity zone. I felt 3D again. The light grew brighter and brighter until we finally made ourselves back into the lab. The Wormhole behind us closed and a heavy smoke started coming from it. I was in the 3D world again. The others were shocked to see me and the Lab again, until they fainted because of gravity. Well, I saw them faint and then I did for 2 reasons. I was really tired, and I felt that there was something pulling me so hard, and I couldn't bare it.

I woke up in the lab and my grandfather was hovering above me.

"Good heavens it is so good to see you."

"You too I managed to say."

"I thought you were gone. I persisted to keep the hole open

in case you ever came. I almost lost hope."

"Why is that."

"Did you forget. Time dilation. How long did you spend there?"

"Around an hour I suppose."

"Well that is around a year and a half."

"Wow. Thanks for holding the hole open."

"You really did a good job kiddo." "Where are my parents and James?"

"I have informed your stepparents, and they will reach any time along with James. He got his driver's licence a few days ago."

"What he's fourteen."

"Not anymore. He is 16 and so are you."

"But how I thought I won't be affected."

"You were in the 4th dimension, so you had the chance of actually aging in that One hour."

"What!"

"Yes you did. Look at the mirror."

I did look at it. I seemed the same just a little taller and a little older.

"How about my biological parents and the other people who came along with them?" "They have been under medical observation since they all have been too long out there. But don't worry they are fine and waiting to meet you. Your stepparents met them at the hospital too. Your family has just grown bigger. Oh, here comes James and your stepparents." smiled grandfather.

Both my stepmom and stepdad hugged me tightly and shed tears of joy after reuniting with me. Kate looked happy too and that surprised me.

James came up to me. Gave me a fist bump. He did look the same but again taller and older.

"How are you doing!?"
"I'm fine. What did you do in those 1 and a half years."
"Practically almost every second here."
"What about school."
"Of course I attended school silly."
"Anyways how are you doing."
"I'm fine just saw the coolest things in the world."
"Sounds exciting. How was the road trip?"
"Good enough. A little bumpy."
"What do you expect a smooth road trip or that aeroplane ride I gave you."
"Your aeroplane ride was terrible."
"It was fine."
"Imagine we landed."
"Except that part it was totally normal absolutely no problems."
"Yea for sure. The plane landed smoothly."
"You won't believe it Ceser is appointed here now."
"That's nice."
"And here's a surprise for you."
"What is it?"
"Close your eyes."
"Ok now open them."
I opened it to see one of the cutest golden retriever puppies in the world. Its tail was wagging, and it jumped on me the moment it saw me.
"I think it likes me."
"Or trying to tenderize you."
"Or both."
"No I think it likes you."
"What do I name him? It is Max."
"That is a nice name. At least it's not Albert. Talking of whom where is he."

"In jail", said grandfather.
"Sounds fun. Lucky him."
"You seem to really like Max."
"Yes I do."
"It was a gift from Ceser when she heard that you came."
"How did she know that I love dogs."
"Why didn't you sit in the back seat that day."
"I'm sure that wasn't a dog."
"By the way Doodle Doo gave birth to 3 puppies."
"Let me guess neither of them know how to get up."
"How did you know?"
"It was pretty much obvious."

CHAPTER FOURTEEN

T minus 30
initializing all launch procedures
"Navigation communication!"
"Check chief."
"Climate holder."
"Check."
"Connection."
"Check
"Fuel booster temperature."
"-100 on the outside."
"Rocket is good to go. I repeat good to go"
T minus
10
9
8
7
6
"Main Engine booster fire."
5
4
3
2
"Thrust acquired."

1

"Engine ignition."

"We have liftoff."

"Lift off is normal I repeat liftoff is normal."

There was a roar of claps from all around the mission control centre. We watched as the Gregarious lifted off from Earth and soared high above the sky.

"Stage one booster number 3 and 4 separation."

There was pin drop silence in the room."

"Stage one completed. Stage 2 booster number 1,2,5,6 separation."

"Stage 2 normal."

There was still tension in the room.

"Stage 3 separation."

The whole crowd looked up to see the animation of 1/4th of the rocket gets separated from another. The rest of the rocket did not budge. The tension grew and slowly the fire of the engine was seen, and the rocket started moving again.

"Stage 3 completed."

After few minutes the 4 and 5th stages started to separate. And finally, we could see the orb of energy. It would explode at the centre of the Universe and produce enough energy for the universe to keep expanding. Now we just had to dock it into the slingshot. We watched as the docker started moving closer and closer to its destination. As we saw it dock we saw the energy transfer of the orb. It started glowing white. A holy circle. The energy transfer would take 2 months.

Fast forward 2 months and the orb's energy light was now seen from Earth it was bright. It was like another moon in the sky. The day had come, and we would sling shot it at 30% of the speed of light. The more it accelerated the faster it went. It was literally bending the laws of physics. Light travelled slower than it should. The Orb started being spun around like a centrifuge and its kinetic Energy grew so much that after 10 rounds, we released, and it flew into space. The faster it went the brighter it went. We ran outside to see the orb grow so bright it practically covered the entire sky and the light slowly started to fade. The speed of it was seen in the computer and the amount of energy it had and was releasing was so great that the computer almost crashed. In a few seconds the ball would explode and there were waves of energy and momentum throughout the Universe and the Great countdown began. The world was counting on this moment. I saw the computer and it was the last 10 seconds and I knew that the universe would be saved as all the memories of everything it was all because of a great force. A comforting force. It was truly great. It finally happened as the orb exploded and energy travelling a trillion times the speed of light and a wave of light appeared in the sky. It was like the aurora borealis. It was a beautiful blue wave. It was like the sky became an ocean.

"We finally saved the universe right Kurg."

"Yes James we did."

"Sit down Max."

"Good boy."

Max happily wagged his tail with his tongue outside. I picked him up and started petting him. Doodle doo and her puppies came up to us. Max Jumped out of my hand and onto the ground where he and the other puppies started playing and giving small barks. I looked up and saw the light of energy slowly fade away to reappear brighter again. My biological dad came up to me and tapped me and James on the shoulder.

"Good job guys we finally brought the universe to stability."

"We did."

I was happy about this mission. My Parents got to know my stepparents and now they are happy that I am part of Eureka.

"Do you ever wonder if we didn't notice the clock."

"Yea I do wonder that and I think we would be here anyways."

"Why do you think that."

"The force that took us here."

"And what is that."

"The Next dimension."

"That's a nice name."

"It is, isn't it?"

We slowly watched as the lights slowly faded forever and the sun slowly set revealing the starts in the night sky."

"It really is beautiful isn't it."

"It is."

"The riddle of the Universe."

THE END

About The Author

Pranav Sunil

Pranav Sunil is a 12-year-old student at a prominent school in Bangalore, India. He is a very creative child who loves to spend his free time drawing, painting, and most of all reading. His interest in reading began at a very young age and his favorite genre was fantasy. He is also a space enthusiast, a repeated Astronomy Olympiad winner and dreams of becoming an astrophysicist one day. Until then he wants to try his hands at writing thriller and sci-fi books for children.

Tales of Terror was his first book which he has authored.

84

9 7 9 8 8 9 4 1 5 8 1 3 6